My Cousin Tamar
Lives in Israel

Michelle Shapiro Abraham

Illustrated by Ann D. Koffsky

URJ Press   ✦   New York

To our Jewish Homeland, the Land of Israel,
the place where I met my husband and that
I look forward to sharing with my children.
May the joyful sounds of singing and
holiday celebration forever fill Her streets.

MSA

For Amalia, Amitai, Ezra, and Joshua.

MDK

Library of Congress Cataloging-in-Publication Data

Abraham, Michelle Shapiro.
   My cousin Tamar lives in Israel / Michelle Shapiro Abraham ;
illustrated by Ann D. Koffsky.
        p. cm.
   Summary: A boy living in the United States describes differences
in the way he and his family observe Jewish traditions, and the
way his cousin and her family observe the same traditions in
the Jewish homeland.
   ISBN-13: 978-0-8074-0989-3 (alk. paper)
   ISBN-10: 0-8074-0989-8 (alk. paper)
   [1. Judaism—Customs and practices—Fiction. 2. Jews—Israel—
Fiction.]   I. Koffsky, Ann D., ill.   II. Title.
   PZ7.A16592My 2007
   [E]—dc22   2007051498

This book is printed on acid-free paper.
Copyright ©2007 by URJ Press
Manufactured in the United States of America
10 9 8 7 6 5 4 3 2 1

This is my
home.

This is my cousin
Tamar's home.
My cousin Tamar
lives in Jerusalem.
Jerusalem is in
Israel.

On Shabbat in my home, when we sing the candle blessings we know that Shabbat has begun.

On Shabbat in Israel, Tamar hears the Shabbat horn telling the whole city Shabbat has begun!

On Yom Kippur, when my family goes to synagogue
we walk past open stores and cars speeding by.

On Yom Kippur in Israel, Tamar walks to services past closed stores and there is hardly a car on the road at all!

On Sukkot in my home, we eat in our backyard sukkah or at the synagogue.

On Sukkot in Israel, Tamar eats in a sukkah
everywhere she goes!

On Chanukah in my home, we fry latkes on my kitchen stove.

On Chanukah in Israel, Tamar buys *sufganiyot*, fried jelly donuts, from the stand in the street.

On Purim in my home, I dress up in a costume and go to temple
for the megillah reading and costume parade.

On Purim in Israel, Tamar and her friends wear their costumes all day long, and even the bus drivers dress up!

On Passover in my home, we make matzah pizza for the whole family.

On Passover in Israel, Tamar's favorite restaurant
makes matzah pizza for everyone!

I live in a Jewish home.

My cousin Tamar lives in Israel—the Jewish Homeland.